To Parents

Farmyard, pet and wild animals are all included
in this delightful collection of familiar and
not so familiar animals.

Help children to develop reading and language
skills by looking through the book together.
Encourage them to look closely at the pictures,
spot similarities and differences, and
to talk about what they see.
Children will soon learn to recognise
the animals and enjoy matching
the names to the pictures.

A catalogue record for this book is available
from the British Library

Published by Ladybird Books Ltd
A subsidiary of the Penguin Group
A Pearson Company
© LADYBIRD BOOKS LTD MCMXCIII

LADYBIRD and the device of a Ladybird are trademarks of
Ladybird Books Ltd Loughborough Leicestershire UK

First
animal
words

illustrated by LYNNE FARMER

Ladybird

dogs

puppy

cats

kittens

rabbit

mouse

hamster

budgerigars

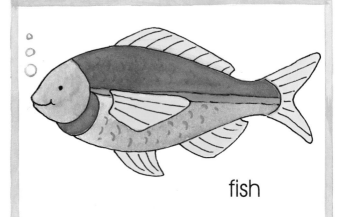

fish

guinea pig

peacock

owl

penguins

walrus

whale

dolphins

horse

foal

cow

calf

sheep

lambs

pig

piglets

chicken

chicks

cockerel

goat

kid

duck

ducklings

drake

elephant

panda

lion

lion cub

lioness

tiger

parrot

giraffe

toucan

snake

bear

hippopotamus

kangaroo

joey

koala

camel

turtle

bear

budgerigars
calf
camel
cats
chicken
chicks
cockerel
cow
dogs
dolphins

drake
duck

ducklings
elephant
fish
foal
giraffe
goat
guinea pig

hamster
hippopotamus
horse
joey
kangaroo